Parables in action

5

Cooks, Cakes, and Chocolate Shakes

W9-CEK-064

By Nancy I. Sanders
and Susan Titus Osborn

CPH.
SAINT LOUIS

Illustrated by Ronda Krum

With love for my granddaughter Taylor.
May you learn more about Jesus
through reading this book. — S.T.O.

With love for Janice and Bob Shaner.
Thanks for your example of living
and knowing Jesus. — N.I.S.

Parables in Action Series

Lost and Found
Hidden Treasure
Comet Campout
Moon Rocks and Dinosaur Bones
Cooks, Cakes, and Chocolate Shakes
The Super-Duper Seed Surprise

Text copyright © 2000 Nancy I. Sanders and Susan Titus Osborn
Illustrations copyright © 2000 Concordia Publishing House

Published by Concordia Publishing House
3558 S. Jefferson Avenue, St. Louis, MO 63118-3968
Manufactured in the United States of America

1 2 3 4 5 6 7 8 9 10   09 08 07 06 05 04 03 02 01 00

Hi! My name is Suzie. Today is extra special. It's my teacher's birthday. His name is Mr. Zinger. And Mr. Zinger's the best.

My friends are coming to my house. We are going to make a birthday cake for Mr. Zinger.

Ding! Dong! The doorbell rang. I opened the door. There stood my friend Mario and his dog. "Hi, Mario!" I said. "Hi, Woof!"

Woof wagged his tail and barked. "WOOF!"

"Hi, Suzie," said Mario. "I brought the flour to make the birthday cake."

"Great," I said. "It's going to be an extra special, super-duper cake. The best cake ever!"

Just then Bubbles walked up. Bubbles carried a bag of sugar. She was dressed like a bride. She wore a long white dress and pretty white gloves.

"Are you going to help bake the cake?" Mario asked Bubbles. "Won't you get dirty in that dress?"

"I'll be careful," Bubbles said. "I have to practice being a bride. It's for my next TV ad—*Just Married Amanda*. Amanda's a doll. She dresses up like a bride."

Bubbles does ads on TV. She always practices for them.

Mario and I walked into the kitchen. Bubbles followed slowly. She looked like a real bride. She took tiny steps down the hall. She gave me the bag of sugar.

6

7

Ding! Dong! The doorbell rang
again.

Woof barked. "WOOF!"

"That's The Spy," I said. "Will
you open the door, please, Mario?"

Mario opened the door. Bubbles
and I got the bowls and spoons.

The Spy walked into the
kitchen. He looked at the flour.
He looked at the sugar. He
opened his spy book. He wrote
down spy notes. The Spy always
wrote spy notes.

9

"Why didn't The Spy bring anything? Will he help make the cake?" Mario asked.

"He brought the recipe," I said. "It's the most important part!"

The Spy let me peek inside his spy book. I studied the recipe. We wanted to make the cake just right!

SLAM! The Spy shut his book. We were ready to cook. And just in time. The birthday party would start soon!

Zook!
Zook!

Bubbles put sugar into the bowl. Mario put flour into the bowl. I put milk into the bowl. The Spy put his finger into the bowl.

"Zook! Zook!" The Spy said, licking his finger.

I knew what he said. I'd been friends with The Spy for a long time. "Zook! Zook!" was his secret code for "yummy." The Spy liked to talk in secret code.

We mixed. We stirred.
We put the cake mix in a pan.
We popped it into the oven.
Bubbles set the timer.
We all sat down to wait.
The Spy opened his spy book.
He wrote more notes.

GR-R-R-R-R.

"What was that noise?"
I asked. "Was that Woof?"

GR-R-R-R-R. I heard it
again!

"No," Mario said. "It's my
tummy. All this cooking has
made me hungry. Can we
cook something for us?"

I shook my head. "I don't
know how to cook," I said.
"That's why we're using The
Spy's recipe. But I'm hungry
too."

I peeked over The Spy's shoulder. I saw another recipe in his spy book! A recipe for chocolate shakes.

"Wow!" I said. "Chocolate shakes! That sounds yummy. Can we use that recipe too?"

The Spy nodded his head. He showed us the recipe.

"Let's make chocolate shakes," Bubbles said. "I'm hungry three."

We all laughed at the joke.

18

I put in the milk.
Mario put in the ice cream.
Bubbles put in the chocolate.
The Spy put in his finger.
"Zook! Zook!" The Spy said,
licking his finger.

Soon we were all drinking
chocolate shakes. The Spy was
right. They were yummy!

BEEP! BEEP! BEEP! BEEP!
The timer rang.

Woof jumped up. He was sleeping under the table.

"WOOF! WOOF! WOOF! WOOF!"

The Spy shut his spy book. SLAM!

"Hey!" Mario yelled. "The cake is done! The extra special, super-duper birthday cake is done!"

V-E-R-Y carefully, we pulled the cake out of the oven. We wore oven mitts. We put the cake on the table. We looked at it.
It wasn't a super-duper cake.
It was small. It was flat. It was hard.

V-E-R-Y carefully, The Spy
pulled off a bite with a spoon.
He licked the spoon. He shook
his head. "Blaat," he said.

I knew what he said. "Blaat"
was The Spy's secret code for
"yucky."

"This cake looks terrible!"
Bubbles said. "I'm going to cry!
But I can't cry today. I'm prac-
ticing to be a bride. Brides are
happy. What are we going to
do?"

I knew what to do.

"Let's pray," I said.

I grabbed her hand. Mario
grabbed The Spy's hand. We all
held hands and prayed.

26

We asked Jesus to help us
know what to do. We wanted
to make a special cake. We
wanted to show how special
Mr. Zinger was! And it was
almost time for the party!

27

The Spy opened his book. He wrote more spy notes. I peeked in his book. I saw the recipe for the cake.

"What's yeast?" I asked.

"Yeast?" Mario said. "I don't know."

"I know what it is," Bubbles said. "Yeast is something you cook with. I did a cooking ad for TV once. We used yeast to make bread. The bread was fluffy and soft."

I looked at The Spy's book. "I think we made a mistake. We forgot to add the yeast."

Bubbles shook her head. "Are you sure cakes need yeast?"

The Spy showed her his spy book.

She pointed to the recipe. "Yes. This recipe says to add yeast. Some cakes need yeast to be fluffy and soft too."

I said a quick prayer. I
thanked Jesus for His help.

"It's almost time for the
party," said Mario. "Can we
make it?"

"Let's try!" I shouted.

31

32

Bubbles put sugar in the bowl. Mario put flour in the bowl. I put milk in the bowl. Then I added the yeast. The Spy put his finger in the bowl.

"Zook! Zook!" The Spy said, licking his finger.

"Hurry!" Bubbles cried.

We popped the cake into the oven.

We waited and waited for the timer to ring.

Bubbles practiced walking slowly across the floor. She looked like a real bride.

The Spy wrote more notes in his spy book.

I watched the clock. Would the cake be done in time?

35

BEEP! BEEP! BEEP! BEEP!
The timer rang.

Woof jumped up. He'd been
sleeping under the table again.

"WOOF! WOOF! WOOF!
WOOF!"

The Spy shut his spy book.
SLAM!

We ran to the oven. We
turned it off. V-E-R-Y carefully
we opened the door. We looked
inside.

38

"Wow!" Mario shouted.
"Look! The yeast worked!"

"That's the most beautiful
cake in the world!" Bubbles
said. "It looks like a wedding
cake! It's the biggest cake I've
ever seen!"

We pulled out the cake. We
put it on the table. Mario gave
The Spy a high five. I grabbed
Bubbles' gloves. We jumped up
and down and shouted.

"It's the biggest and the
best! It's an extra special,
super-duper cake all right!"
I shouted.

The Spy reached out. He took
a little bite. He licked his finger.
"Zook! Zook!"

Woof wagged his tail. "WOOF!"

"Hip, hip, hooray!" we cheered.

"Let's take the cake to the
birthday party," I said. "Hurry!
It's time for the party to start."

We ran to the party just in time.

We all started to sing "Happy Birthday" to Mr. Zinger. There was enough cake for the whole school!

43

Parable of the Yeast

Based on Matthew 13:33

One day, Jesus told a parable: "God's kingdom is like yeast," He said.

"When yeast is mixed with flour to make bread, it is fluffy and tastes good. Without the yeast, bread becomes hard and dry."

The cake Suzie and her friends baked was like that bread. It needed yeast to be fluffy and to taste good.

When we believe that Jesus is our Savior, we're part of His kingdom. Just like yeast helps bake good bread, Jesus helps us do things for others that show His love. He helps us be extra special, super-duper too!

46

47

Hi, everyone! God wants you and your friends to be part of His kingdom. He wants you to believe in Jesus and ask Him to help you do kind and loving things. Here's one way you can put Jesus' Parable of the Yeast into ACTION!

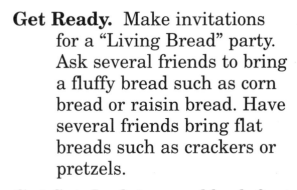

Parables In Action

Get Ready. Make invitations for a "Living Bread" party. Ask several friends to bring a fluffy bread such as corn bread or raisin bread. Have several friends bring flat breads such as crackers or pretzels.

Get Set. Look in a cookbook for a recipe for milk shakes. Make enough for your party.

Go! Have fun with your friends at the party tasting the different breads and drinking shakes. Watch a video about when Jesus fed the 5,000.